Fear Not, Sweet Frances

Written & Illustrated by Arin Guthe

fear not little firefly
your light was meant to show
to be A lamp upon the path
with just the perfect glow.

so shine your light for everyone
And do not hide your Beauty
it's a gift for all travelers here
And such a noble duty.

fear not little tiny frog
for this you need to know,
that life brings change and PURPOSE
You will see this as you grow.

If you feel Ashamed or sad

I'm right here by your side

Reminding you of who you are

That grace will be your guide.

fear not little nimble fish

your eyes are sharp to see

the shadows that are light and dark

whose patterns dance for me.

so when you want to hide your face
Remember I am here
to comfort you in every way
my love is most sincere.

fear not little feathered finch

you have no need to long

Nothing more brings me joy

Than to hear your morning song.

You Have Everything You Need

So when the snow and winter come
and food is hard to find

do trust me with your nest and seed

for this is by design.

fear not the dark gentle fox
where you are meant to dwell

in the joy and life with others

that come to love you well.

When you feel confused or worried

And nothing seems quite right

Remember I created you

I walk with you through the night.

YOU ARE NOT ALONE

fear not little spotted fawn

You too Are loved and known

The grass will grow and seasons change

But you Are not alone.

If you find yourself alone or sad

Remember I am near

I'll comfort, care and stand with you

I will not disappear.

You are mine

fear not my sweet, sweet Frances

You are truly meant to be

Brave and Strong and nestled close

Right here next to me.

So while Big Storms will come and go

And the wind and Rain appear

You, my love will be held close

Sweet Frances, do not fear.

See All these things, the light, the grace

the love you seek to find

All are here, come follow me.

I offer peace of mind.

So walk on through this creation

And think on all you've found

I knew you before you were you

I will not let you down.

Fear Not, Sweet Frances
Fear Not.

The End

Trade the fear FOR Truth

i Am Afraid of....

| the DARK | You are a Light. Matthew 5:14 |

| CHANGE | You have purpose. Romans 8:28 |

| being ALONE | You are not alone. Deuteronomy 31:6 |

NOT HAVING WHAT i NEED

You have everything you need.
Luke 12:24

things UNSEEN

You are seen.
Hebrews 11:1

OTHERS

You are loved.
Psalm 139

things i CANNOT CONTROL

You are mine.
Isaiah 43:1

Each 'truth' is based on a biblical scripture verse.
Take time a look up each verse.

About the Author + illustrator

Arin is the artist and owner of True Cotton - an art, illustration and papergoods company. True Cotton is full of whimsy and a place where hope lands on paper.

She draws inspiration from nature - mostly in the spot where the forest meets the wild flower blooms. She and her husband have the daily adventure of raising four children, and living out the gospel in real time.

Find her online
INSTAGRAM - @truecottonart
WWW.TRUE-COTTON.COM

Life can be full of really hard moments, times where we are afraid, anxious, sad, insecure, worried, stressed, mad, hurt, confused or lonely.

We are not created to stay stuck in our fears. Isn't this amazing news? There's Hope!

It isn't God's intention for us to hide and allow these fears to take over. He's given us a pathway to speak to him. He made it possible for us to have a way to talk with him, no matter where we are. You see, Jesus is God's son, and they are perfect. Us - well, we are a mess. God sent Jesus to become part of our mess, died on a cross for all that mess, called sin, he rose from the grave - giving us a pathway to have a friendship with God.

So what do we do now, that we have this friendship with God? This part, it's on us. We have the chance to chat with God. And even though he knows what's going on, we get to talk to him in prayer. This talking can sound a lot like a conversation between friends. God's word, the Bible, is full of calls to prayer. In seasons of sadness, joy, thankfulness and yes, absolutely about our fears. (Psalm 34:4)

So now it's your turn! When you feel overwhelmed, sad, discouraged or lonely, talk to God about everything that's going on. Tell him! Say it out loud if you have to. Tell Him you're not gonna carry all your fears on your own.

He's got you! Trust Him.
He promises to be with you every step of the way.

Prayer

God, thank you for today. Help me to remember you see me, know me, love me and will never leave me. Give me courage in my all fears. Help me to be still, slow down and look at all you've created around me. Give me strength to hand you the things I am worried about. I can't carry them on my own. Give me peace as I trust you in the unknown. Thank you for loving me so much.

AMEN

this sweet book is dedicated to...

our 'Boof'. You are wide-eyed and full of light. You are our songbird, who's melody brings such life to our home. In the mystery of parenting, God has forged the most surprising and beautiful lessons on our hearts, through you. May you always know who you are. May you listen to your Creator's voice when the path isn't clear. May He give you peace as you trust Him in the unknown. May you surrender the things you can't control. He is before you, with you and behind you, and so are we!

You are so dearly loved.

ISBN: 9781687774309

Contact Arin - truecottonart@gmail.com
Instagram @truecottonart

1st printing.

Fear Not,
for i HAVE
REdEEMed
You; i HAVE called
you BY NAME,
You ARE
Mine

~isaiah 43:1~

true cotton

Fear Not

All my love.
xo

Made in the USA
Lexington, KY
07 November 2019